T0361481

A FEW RULES FOR PREDICTING THE FUTURE

OCTAVIA E. BUTLER

A FEW RULES FOR PREDICTING THE FUTURE

An Essay

ART BY MANZEL BOWMAN

CHRONICLE BOOKS
SAN FRANCISCO

Text copyright © 2000 by Octavia E. Butler.

First Chronicle Books LLC edition, published in 2024.
Originally published in *Essence* magazine; May 2000;
31, 1; pp. 164–66.

All rights reserved. No part of this book may be repro-
duced in any form without written permission from the
publisher.

Library of Congress Cataloging-in-Publication Data
available.

ISBN 978-1-7972-2905-8

Manufactured in China.

MIX
Paper | Supporting
responsible forestry
FSC™ C136333

Design by Allison Weiner.
Cover lettering by Abigail Dahl.

10 9 8 7 6 5 4 3 2

Chronicle books and gifts are available at special
quantity discounts to corporations, professional associ-
ations, literacy programs, and other organizations. For
details and discount information, please contact our
corporate/premiums department at corporatesales@
chroniclebooks.com or at 1-800-759-0190.

Chronicle Books LLC
680 Second Street
San Francisco, California 94107
www.chroniclebooks.com

"So do you really believe that in the future we're going to have the kind of trouble you write about in your books?" a student asked me as I was signing books after a talk. The young man was referring to the troubles I'd described in *Parable of the Sower* and *Parable of the Talents*, novels that take place in a near future of increasing drug addiction and illiteracy, marked by the popularity of prisons and the unpopularity of public schools, the vast and growing gap between the rich and everyone else, and the whole nasty family of problems brought on by global warming.

"I didn't make up the problems," I pointed out. "All I did was look around at the problems we're neglecting now and give them about 30 years to grow into full-fledged disasters."

"Okay," the young man challenged. "So what's the answer?"

"There isn't one," I told him.

"No answer? You mean we're just doomed?" He smiled as though he thought this might be a joke.

"No," I said. "I mean there's no single answer that will solve all of our future problems. There's no magic bullet. Instead there are thousands of answers—at least. You can be one of them if you choose to be."

Several days later, by mail, I received a copy of the young man's story in his college newspaper. He mentioned my talk, listed some of my books and the future problems they dealt with. Then he quoted his own question: "What's the answer?" The article ended with the first three words of my reply, wrongly left standing alone: "There isn't one."

It's sadly easy to reverse meaning, in fact, to tell a lie, by offering an accurate but incomplete quote. In this case, it was frustrating because the one thing that I and my main characters never do when contemplating the future is give up hope. In fact, the very act of trying to look ahead to discern possibilities and offer warnings is in itself an act of hope.

LEARN FROM THE PAST

Of course, writing novels about the future doesn't give me any special ability to foretell the future. But it does encourage me to use our past and present behaviors as guides to the kind of world we seem to be creating. The past, for example, is filled with repeating cycles of strength and weakness, wisdom and stupidity, empire and ashes. To study history is to study humanity. And to try to foretell the future without studying history is like trying to learn to read without bothering to learn the alphabet.

When I was preparing to write *Parable of the Talents*, I needed to think about how a country might slide into fascism—something that America does in *Talents*. So I reread *The Rise and Fall of the Third Reich* and other books on Nazi Germany. I was less interested in the fighting of World War II than in the prewar story of how Germany changed as it suffered social and economic problems, as Hitler and others bludgeoned and seduced, as the Germans responded to the bludgeoning and the seduction and to their own history, and as Hitler used that history to manipulate them.

I wanted to understand the lies that people have to tell themselves when they either quietly or joyfully watch their neighbors ruined, spirited away, killed. Different versions of this horror have happened again and again in history. They're still happening in places like Rwanda, Bosnia, Kosovo and East Timor, wherever one group of people permits its leaders to convince them that for their own protection, for the safety of their families and the security of their country, they must *get* their enemies, those alien others who until now were their neighbors.

It's easy enough to spot this horror when it happens elsewhere in the world or elsewhere in time. But if we are to spot it here at home, to spot it before it can grow and do its worst, we must pay more attention to history. This came home to me a few years ago, when I lived across the street from a 15-year-old girl whose grandfather asked me to help her with homework. The girl was doing a report on a man who had fled Europe during the 1930s because of some people called—she hesitated and then pronounced a word that was clearly unfamiliar to her—"the Nayzees?" It took me a moment to realize that she meant the Nazis, and that she knew absolutely nothing about them. We forget history at our peril.

RESPECT THE LAW OF CONSE-QUENCES

Just recently I complained to my doctor that the medicine he prescribed had a very annoying side effect.

"I can give you something to counteract that," my doctor said.

"A medicine to counteract the effects of another medicine?" I asked.

He nodded. "It will be more comfortable for you."

I began to backpedal. I *hate* to take medicine. "The problem isn't that bad," I said. "I can deal with it."

"You don't have to worry," my doctor said. "This second medication works and there are no side effects."

That stopped me. It made me absolutely certain that I didn't want the second medicine. I realized that I didn't believe there were any medications that had no side effects. In fact, I don't believe we can do anything at all without side effects— also known as unintended consequences. Those consequences may be beneficial or harmful. They may be too slight to matter or they may be worth the risk because the potential benefits are great, but the consequences are always there. In *Parable of the Sower*, my character put it this way:

All that you touch
You Change

All that you Change
Changes you

The only lasting truth
Is Change

God
Is Change

BE
AWARE OF
YOUR
PERSPECTIV

How many combinations of unintended consequences and human reactions to them does it take to detour us into a future that seems to defy any obvious trend? Not many. That's why predicting the future accurately is so difficult.

Some of the most mistaken predictions I've seen are of the straight-line variety— that's the kind that ignores the inevitability of unintended consequences, ignores our often less-than-logical reactions to them, and says simply, "In the future, we will have more and more of whatever's holding our attention right now." If we're in a period of prosperity, then in the future, prosperity it will be. If we're in a period of recession, we're doomed to even greater distress.

Of course, predicting an impossible state of permanent prosperity may well be an act of fear and superstitious hope rather than an act of unimaginative, straight-line thinking. And predicting doom in difficult times may have more to do with the sorrow and depression of the moment than with any real insight into future possibilities. Superstition, depression and fear play major roles in our efforts at prediction.

It's also true that where we stand determines what we're able to see. Where I stood when I began to pay attention to space travel certainly influenced what I saw. I followed the space race of the late 1950s and the 1960s not because it was a race, but because it was taking us away from Earth, away from home, away to investigate the mysteries of the universe and, I thought, to find new homes for humanity out there. This appealed to me, at least in part, because I was in my teens and beginning to think of leaving my mother's house and investigating the mysteries of my own adulthood.

Apollo 11 reached the moon in July 1969. I had already left home by then, and I believed I was watching humanity leave home. I assumed that we would go on to establish lunar colonies and eventually send people to Mars. We probably will do those things someday, but I never imagined that it would take as long as it has. Moral: Wishful thinking is no more help in predicting the future than fear, superstition or depression.

COUNT ON THE SURPRISES

I was speaking to a group of college students not long ago, and I mentioned the fear we'd once had of nuclear war with the Soviet Union. The kids I was talking to were born around 1980, and one of them spoke up to say that she had never worried about nuclear war. She had never believed that such a thing could possibly happen— she thought the whole idea was nonsense.

She could not imagine that during the Cold War days of the sixties, seventies and eighties, no one would have dared to predict a peaceful resolution in the nineties. I remembered air-raid drills when I was in elementary school, how we knelt, heads down against corridor walls with our bare hands supposedly protecting our bare necks, hoping that if nuclear war ever happened, Los Angeles would be spared. But the threat of nuclear war is gone, at least for the present, because to our surprise our main rival, the Soviet Union, dissolved itself. No matter how hard we try to foresee the future, there are always these surprises. The only safe prediction is that there always will be.

So why try to predict the future at all if it's so difficult, so nearly impossible? Because making predictions is one way to give warning when we see ourselves drifting in dangerous directions. Because prediction is a useful way of pointing out safer, wiser courses. Because, most of all, our tomorrow is the child of our today. Through thought and deed, we exert a great deal of influence over this child, even though we can't control it absolutely. Best to think about it, though. Best to try to shape it into something good. Best to do that for any child.

OCTAVIA E. BUTLER (1947–2006) was a pioneering science fiction writer whose groundbreaking novels, which reflect on racial injustice, women's rights, environmental collapse, and political disparity, include *Kindred*, *Wild Seed*, and *Parable of the Sower*. She was the first African American woman to win a Hugo Award and the first African American woman to win a Nebula Award. She was the first science fiction author to be awarded a MacArthur Fellowship and, in the year 2000, was the recipient of a PEN American Lifetime Achievement Award. Today, her books are taught in over 200 colleges and universities.